THE CURIOUS SC

CU00940480

"The brilliant and entertaining illustrations in this series enliven a clear and enjoyable text that should stimulate serious thought about the world and our place in it."

LORD REES
Astronomer Royal, President of the Royal Society 2005–2010

"Too often science and faith are pitted against each other. This book breaks down that split in a creative and engaging way. It shows the scope of science in our lives and how the study of science and the study of God feed and magnify each other. Human beings have always been hungry for understanding and meaning, and this book beautifully shows how this has worked out from the earliest time. It is a book that leaves me in awe at the 'art' of science: for the way it unveils the magnificence of God our Creator, who stretches out the canvas."

MOST REVEREND JUSTIN WELBY
Archbishop of Canterbury

"A witty and accessible treasure trove of scientific discoveries that goes to the heart of our human quest to understand who we are. This book doesn't dumb down or gloss over imponderables but will leave you marvelling at the science and asking for more."

PROFESSOR REBECCA FITZGERALD
Director of Medical Studies, University of Cambridge
Lister Prize Fellowship (2008), NHS Innovation (2011), NIHR
Research Professorship (2013)

"Has the bug bitten you? Are you curious? Curious to know how the universe evolved from the Big Bang? How matter arranges itself into objects ranging from atomic nuclei to human beings, planets,

and stars? Are you curious to know why all these things are the way they are?

Science is good for the 'how' questions but does not necessarily have the answers on the 'why' questions. Can science and religion talk to each other? Enjoy this series and learn more about science and the enriching dialogue between science and faith."

PROFESSOR ROLF HEUER
Director General of CERN from 2009 to 2015
President of the German Physical Society and President of the
SESAME Council

"Here is a wonderful and wittily written introduction to science as the art of asking open questions and not jumping to conclusions. It's also an amusing excursion through evolution and anthropology which packs in a lot of learning with the lightest of touches. A much-needed antidote to the bludgeoning crudity of so much writing in both science and religion."

REVEREND DOCTOR MALCOLM GUITE
Poet, singer-songwriter, priest, and academic
Chaplain at Girton College Cambridge

THE CURIOUS SCIENCE QUEST

GREEK ADVENTURE

WHO WERE THE FIRST SCIENTISTS?

JULIA GOLDING

WITH ANDREW BRIGGS AND ROGER WAGNER

ILLUSTRATIONS BRETT HUDSON

LION
CHILDREN'S

Published by Lion Children's Books
an imprint of
Lion Hudson Limited
Wilkinson House, Jordan Hill Business Park, Banbury Road,
Oxford OX2 8DR, England
www.lionhudson.com/lionchildrens
ISBN 978 0 7459 7745 4
e-ISBN 978 07459 7759 1
First edition 2018

Acknowledgments
Special thanks to Ancient Scripts for its Mayan names generator: http://ancientscripts.
com/maya.html (see p. 101)

A catalogue record for this book is available from the British Library

Printed and bound in the UK, June 2018, LH26

CONTENTS

INTRODUCTION

Life is full of big questions; what we might call ultimate questions. In the first part of the Curious Science Quest our intrepid time travellers, Harriet and Milton, explored one of the most important mysteries: When did humans start to ask questions?

They discovered that investigating our place in the world goes back far beyond recorded history. Now they are on a mission to find out the next stage in the development of human curiosity. When did we start to ask what we would now call "scientific questions"? In other words, they need to answer: Who were the first scientists?

Our Time Travelling Guides

Meet our guides to the ultimate questions.

Harriet is a tortoise. She was collected by Charles Darwin on his famous voyage on *The Beagle* (1831–36), which was when he explored the world and saw many things that led him to the Theory of Evolution. Harriet was brought back in his suitcase to England to be the family pet. Because she is a tortoise she can live for a very long time and is well over a hundred.

Harriet

Milton is a cat. He belongs to the famous twentieth century physicist, Erwin Schrödinger, and inspired some of his owner's best ideas. Milton is not very good at making up his mind.

Milton

The word "scientist" only came into use in the nineteenth century. Until then, people used the term "philosopher" or "natural philosopher" for those who liked asking questions about how the world works. Maybe Harriet and Milton took the word with them in their time machine?

Curious Science Quest

Thanks to their owners, Harriet and Milton love science, but they don't always agree. This is a good thing because when scientists argue they test out ideas on each other and refine their thinking. Having seen some curious words over the entrance to a famous laboratory in Cambridge University, Harriet and Milton have decided to go on a quest to find out the answers to as many ultimate questions as they can. In fact they are going to travel in time to see all the important events in the history of science.

The works of the Lord are great,
sought out of all them that have pleasure therein

In this series, you are invited to go with them. But look out for the Curiosity Bug hidden in some intriguing places. See how many you can count. (Answer on p. 127.)

The Curiosity Bug

ADVENTURES IN ANCIENT GREECE

How many miles to Miletus?

Harriet is at the controls of the time machine, checking they have not drifted off course. Milton is washing his paws.

"Harriet, I'm really excited to meet the first scientists. Where are they? Do they wear white coats and have laboratories full of bubbling flasks and wacky experiments?"

"Um, no." Harriet smiles at her friend. "It's really not like that."

"Do they teach in classrooms then, with lots of bored children taking notes and the adventurous ones cooking up stink bombs in the back row?" asks Milton.

"That comes much later," explains Harriet.

Milton pulls a face. "Humpf! So where are you taking me?"

She nudges a lever a little to the left. "I've been thinking about that. I thought we'd start in Greece."

"But you're not sure?" Milton is delighted because he is usually the one that can't make up his mind.

"Milton, you will find that the start of something is rarely clear-cut. It grows out of what went before. That's true of science."

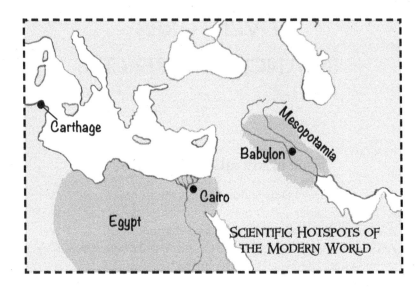

Carthage

Mesopotamia

Babylon

Cairo

Egypt

SCIENTIFIC HOTSPOTS OF
THE MODERN WORLD

SCIENCE BEFORE THE GREEKS

A STAR IS BORN

As Harriet points out, there is no clear-cut beginning to people doing what we now think of as science. Ancient Greece had contacts with many other empires and countries in the region with ships coming and going all the time. The sailors brought not just cargo with them but also the exchange of ideas. Two of the most important links were with the pyramid-building Egyptians and stargazing Mesopotamians (Mesopotamia was the land between the Tigris and Euphrates rivers). A later Greek historian, Herodotus, suggests that the Greeks learnt their astronomy from these nations. One indication of this is that the Greek word for star is "aster" and is thought to come from the name of the Mesopotamian fertility goddess, Ishtar. If the Greeks borrowed that word, the theory is they also borrowed star charts and other astronomical ideas from the Mesopotamians.

ALEPH, BETH, GIMEL, AND DALETH

Another influential civilisation was the Phoenicians who like the Greeks were a trading nation with cities around the Mediterranean. Their most famous centre was Carthage in north Africa. They were known as great sailors, leading the way for Greek sailors to follow. A Greek geographer, Strabo, said the Phoenicians learned stargazing and mathematics to help them chart their course when sailing at night. They also raced against the Greeks to make technical improvements to their vessels, spurring each other on to win trading and battle advantages. But most important of all was their alphabet; a form of which the Greeks borrowed and passed on to the Romans. The first four letters are *aleph*, *beth*, *gimel*, and *daleth*, and the first two of those give us our word for alphabet. We're using the alphabet now in this book, shaking hands with the ancient Phoenicians across time.

TRY THIS AT HOME: BECOME AN ANCIENT MESOPOTAMIAN STARGAZER!

Do you know how to tell the phases of the moon? This is the most basic step to becoming an astronomer like the ancient Mesopotamians. For the next few nights, take a look outside and make a note of the shape of the moon, if you can see it. The first thing you will find is that the moon rises at different times each night, typically 50 minutes later than the night before, so it is best to pick a night when it isn't too late to start your observations. Keep a diary – ideally on days spread across a whole month.

Now you can correctly label these phases of the moon: full, new, full quarter, and third quarter.

 First Quarter

Full Moon

Third Quarter

New Moon

And do you know the difference between waxing and waning? Here's a tip. If it looks like a Ɔ then it is waxing. If it is going from O and gradually thinning to a C then it is waning. If you want to remember this, think "Dogs get bigger; Cats get smaller." That's unless you are reading this in the southern hemisphere. For you the moon does the opposite: Cats bigger; Dogs smaller!

"So tell me what went on before Greek scientists started asking their questions," says Milton. "How did people understand the world around them?"

"You remember we saw big pictures that told stories on the walls of the prehistoric caves?" asks Harriet.

Milton nods. He had particularly liked the pictures of lions drawn by the cave painters.

"At some point before people started to write things down, they also began to make big word pictures, or tales, to explain what happens in the world," explains Harriet. "By the time we reach the Ancient Greeks, they had a whole series of stories explaining events such as thunderstorms and earthquakes. Mostly, they decided it was to do with the actions of gods – beings of great power who could be behind the things they did not understand."

Milton looks out of the porthole to see the stars rushing by. "How much longer until we reach our destination?"

"Quite a while." Harriet, a seasoned traveller, nibbles on her favourite snack of a lettuce leaf.

"Then you'll have time to tell me one of those big stories. I love stories – make it a good one." Milton gets out his own lunch of sardines and prepares to be entertained.

Harriet thinks for a moment, taking a slow swallow to finish her mouthful. She rarely does anything quickly. "I do have a favourite because it explains lots of things all at once: how the sun travels across the sky, what causes an eclipse, and how the deserts of north Africa were formed. Here it is."

Phaethon's Chariot

What causes an eclipse of the sun and made the deserts of north Africa? Let me tell you the story of Phaethon and his disastrous chariot ride.

As any Ancient Greek knows, the passage of the sun across the heavens is due to the god Helios. He drives his shining sun chariot from east to west each day. Helios once came down from the heavens and fell in love with a sea nymph. She bore him a boy called Phaethon, but Helios had to go back to the sky so didn't see his son. Despite this, Phaethon was very proud of his father and boasted about him to anyone who would listen. No one believed his tale and a friend dared him to prove his father really was the sun god. Upset that he was being doubted, Phaethon asked his mother how he could do this. She told him he must go to his father and ask him to allow Phaethon to drive his chariot across the sky so all could see who he was and no more would his claims be questioned.

After a perilous journey across the fertile green plains of Africa, Phaethon found his father's palace. Delighted to meet his son for the first time, Helios swore that he would help Phaethon but when he heard the request, he wished he had not made the vow. No one could drive his chariot without coming to harm, not even the most powerful god, Zeus. However, Helios's word had been given, so the next day Phaethon set off in the chariot with a smart crack of the whip to get the horses moving.

At first, Phaethon loved the feeling it gave him as he soared across the sky in the sun chariot and he urged the horses to go faster. Yet he was no god, and the horses did not respect his hand on the reins. All too soon, Phaethon lost control of the fiery-tempered horses and the sun chariot veered off course, shooting out arcs of flames until it had set the whole of north Africa ablaze. Only the Nile survived the inferno; the rest turned into a scorched desert. Seeing the disaster, Zeus could only end the carnage by throwing a thunderbolt at Phaethon, bringing him and his chariot down from the sky. Phaethon fell in a handful of ashes into the river Po in Italy and the rest of the Earth was saved from the inferno. Grieving for his boy, Helios caught the bolting horses and led them back to their stables. For the rest of the day he did not emerge so there was an eclipse and the world remained in darkness.

"So people thought gods were behind everything?" asks Milton.

Harriet nods. "That's right. It helped them understand the world even if their answer was poetic rather than factual. So when the next thunderstorm came along they could tell themselves not to worry, it was just Zeus in a temper."

"Or that he was blasting Phaethon out of the sky?" suggests Milton.

"Exactly."

Milton thinks for a moment. "So when did people stop thinking like this and start looking for other kinds of answers?"

"Ah, that's why we are going to Greece," says Harriet. "I'm taking you to a very special place. It was where people first started replacing these big stories with an even bigger story that changed the way they thought about the world."

Milton runs through the list of places he has heard of before in that part of the world. "Athens? Delphi where the Oracle lived? Olympia where the games started?"

"No. Miletus."

Milton gives her a grumpy look. "Never heard of it."

"I didn't expect you to. Even at the time wasn't a very important place – not until the people who lived there started thinking. Look, here's a map."

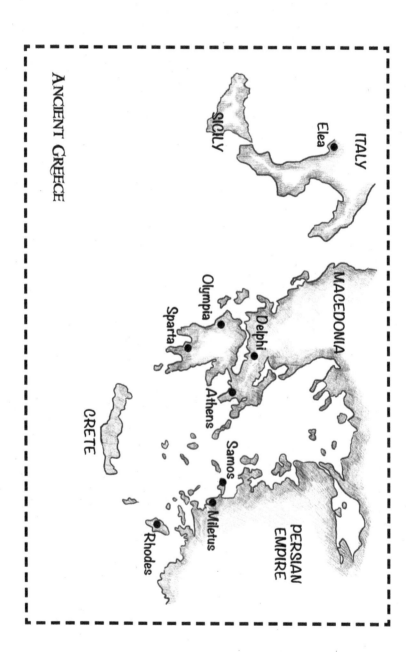

ANCIENT GREECE

SICILY
ITALY
Elea

MACEDONIA
Olympia
Delphi
Sparta
Athens
CRETE
Samos
Miletus
Rhodes
PERSIAN
EMPIRE

"But that's not even in Greece – that's Turkey!" protests Milton.

"It is today but the world looked very different in the year we are visiting, around 600 BC. Many of the countries you know now didn't exist then. Other empires that have been forgotten were in power. Greece itself wasn't a single country but lots of little ones under the sway of different rulers."

"Ah-ha! So why call it Ancient Greece if Greece didn't exist?" asks Milton, thinking he has caught her out.

"Because countries aren't always about what fits inside a national border. The Greeks shared a common language, beliefs in their gods and how to worship them." Harriet dips back into her shell and comes out with a timeline on a scroll. "Here: this should help you understand what happened when in Ancient Greece."

Milton takes it with an impatient flick of his tail. "Know-it-all," he mutters.

850–700
First Greek
alphabet
developed

c. 2500 The Minoan
civilisation flourishes in
Crete until wiped out
(possibly) by a natural
disaster

c. 750–700 Homer
composes his
famous works,
the *Iliad* and the
Odyssey

730–710 The Spartans
conquer south-west
Peloponnese

c. 625 Birth of Thales in
Miletus and beginning of
scientific questioning

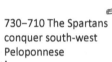

c. 2900
Different
cultures start
to emerge
around the
Mediterranean

776 First Olympic
games

660 Coins
introduced

c. 1200 Collapse of
Mycenaean palace
civilisation

c. 1180 Possible
date for the war
in Troy (if this is
historical)

BC

BRONZE AGE

HOMERIC AGE

RISE OF THE TYRANTS

THE GREEK CLASSICAL PERIOD

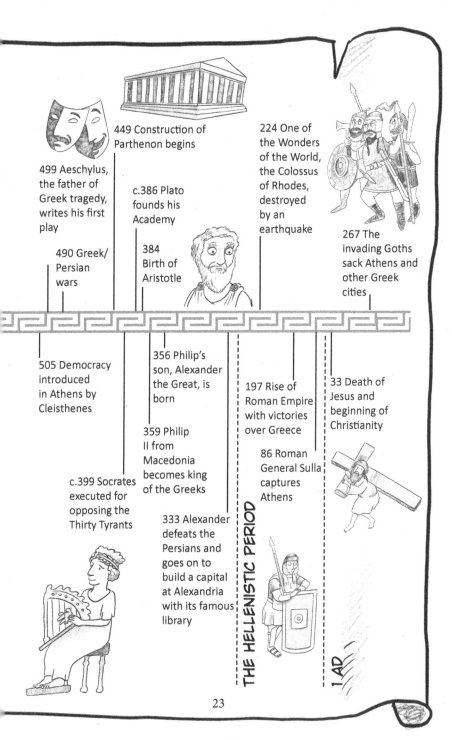

449 Construction of Parthenon begins

499 Aeschylus, the father of Greek tragedy, writes his first play

c.386 Plato founds his Academy

384 Birth of Aristotle

490 Greek/ Persian wars

224 One of the Wonders of the World, the Colossus of Rhodes, destroyed by an earthquake

267 The invading Goths sack Athens and other Greek cities

505 Democracy introduced in Athens by Cleisthenes

356 Philip's son, Alexander the Great, is born

197 Rise of Roman Empire with victories over Greece

33 Death of Jesus and beginning of Christianity

359 Philip II from Macedonia becomes king of the Greeks

86 Roman General Sulla captures Athens

c.399 Socrates executed for opposing the Thirty Tyrants

333 Alexander defeats the Persians and goes on to build a capital at Alexandria with its famous library

THE HELLENISTIC PERIOD

1 AD

23

"Wow, this really is going to be an adventure! This scroll shows us that we are talking about well over a thousand years of history, much of which is guesswork by archaeologists," says Milton.

"Very good guesswork based on evidence, but yes," confirms Harriet. "And many of the scientists we are going to meet we only know about today because fragments of their work are quoted by later thinkers. Scholars have to piece together what the original work was like – a bit like a treasure hunt with most of the clues missing."

Milton pats the control board. "I'm very glad that we have the time machine then."

"Aargh! Watch what you do with your paws, Milton! You almost sent us back to the future!" Harriet corrects their course while Milton sulks in a corner.

The whirling stars fade and Milton perks up when he sees that it is sunny outside.

"I think we've arrived." Harriet opens the door. "While you stopped to catnap earlier, I went ahead to get a friend to round up some of the most interesting scientists from this part of the world so you could meet them all in one go. He used the time machine to bring them together as they were born over a hundred years apart. The oldest is Thales, born around 625 BC; and the youngest is Empedocles, who was born in 495 BC. That is like a biologist from our time meeting Charles Darwin from the nineteenth century."

Milton looks glum. "I'm not sure I can follow all these names."

"Don't worry. My friend Zeno will help us with that," Harriet says, smiling.

"So we are meeting the first scientists?" Milton asks, excitedly. "This is a big moment for me. I think that deserves a fanfare or a drum roll!"

"I can't provide one of those but I can give you a jolly good argument and a chance to vote on your favourite in our 'Greece's Got *Scientific* Talent' contest."

Harriet steps out of the machine and hurries slowly over to a young boy playing with a homemade bow and arrow.

"Hello, Zeno, sorry to keep you waiting." Harriet tweaks at his sandal to get his attention. "Did you manage to find everyone?"

"I did, Harriet. They are waiting for us in the marketplace so they can argue their case and try to win your vote. We Greeks like public votes. You could say we invented them." The boy picks Harriet up and balances her on his shoulder.

Milton purrs, waiting to be stroked.

"And this is your friend Milton, I'm guessing." Zeno rubs Milton under the chin. "Come and see a little of Miletus before we meet the philosophers. We can start here." He puts Harriet down on top of a large statue of a lion, which stands proudly overlooking the many ships being unloaded in the harbour. Milton jumps up on the second statue.

"Out there is the Mediterranean, the sea in between all the countries of the world known to us Greeks. These two lions guard the port," explains Zeno.

"I'm liking this place more and more," says Milton, sitting proudly on the big cat.

"Unfortunately, Milton," says Harriet, "the harbour is silting up so they aren't sure how much longer Miletus will go on being a trading centre. In our day these lions are going to be almost forgotten, sitting well inland covered in undergrowth."

"Pity," mews Milton.

"But I think seeing the sea changing the landscape right before the eyes of local people might have prompted the thinkers to start to ask questions about the forces at play in the world."

"I get it," says Milton. "I remember your story. The locals can see it isn't the god of the sea, Poseidon, in a bad mood, like they might have done once upon a time, but a lot of sand and mud carried into the bay by the Meander River."

"Hey, be careful!" warns Zeno, nudging Milton off his lion. "You can't go around saying that kind of thing out loud! A lot of people are very attached to the gods and don't like thinkers, or what we call philosophers, explaining them away."

"I will keep my lips zipped." Milton mimes the action.

"What's a zip?" asks Zeno.

"Oh, er, never mind," says Milton, shaking his head. "You'll find out later – much, much later."

Zeno fortunately has his mind on other things. "We'd better hurry. Let's go to the marketplace before my friends scatter."

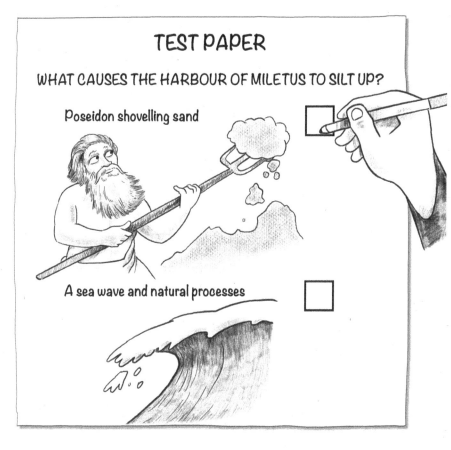

TEST PAPER

WHAT CAUSES THE HARBOUR OF MILETUS TO SILT UP?

Poseidon shovelling sand

A sea wave and natural processes

"Greece's Got *Scientific* Talent" contest

They enter a marketplace where local people meet to exchange goods and news. At the far end by a temple porch is a space for speech-making. Zeno places Harriet on a pillar where she will have a good view of the debate. Milton leaps up beside her.

"Here's the first one right now," says Zeno. "Thales – we call him the Water Man for a soon-to-be-obvious reason. You could also call him the grandaddy of science."

"So what's the first scientific question they ask?" Milton whispers.

"It is a good and logical one: what comes first?" Harriet replies.

Thales   Anaximandros   Anaximenes

A wise-looking elderly man takes his place on a raised platform to address the listeners. "People of Miletus, you don't need to look to the stories of the poets and distant Olympus to explain what is happening in front of you. All things are full of gods. What makes the Earth as it is? Water! Everything is made from it and everything returns to it."

"Water?" Milton whispers to Harriet. "But that isn't a fundamental substance – it's made up of hydrogen and oxygen. Even I know that."

"But the Greeks didn't," Harriet whispers back. "They are making educated guesses as to the building blocks of life. Since every living thing needs water, it's a reasonable guess. Aristotle, whom we'll meet later, called Thales the first rational thinker."

"All right," says Milton, "so that's the grandaddy of science's theory. Let's hear what the next one has to say."

Another man climbs onto the platform.

"This is Anaximandros," explains Zeno.

"Anaxi-what?" asks Milton.

"You can call him Mr Boundless as he doesn't stop talking about things having no limits."

| Pythagoras | Heraclitus | Xenophanes |

Lots of names in Ancient Greece begin with Anax-. There's a reason for this. In Ancient Greek it means "king" or "leader" so it is an impressive name to give a son.

"With respect to my learned colleague, Thales, I have to disagree," shouts Anaximandros. "We have to look beyond water to the boundless, to the origin of everything, to the first cause, or beginning. And that beginning is limitless so it will carry on creating things without end."

| Parmenides | Empedocles | Anaxagoras |

MEET THE SCIENTIST

ANAXIMANDROS, MR BOUNDLESS

- Lived: c. 610–546 BC
- Number of jobs: 1 (philosopher)
- Influence (out of 100): 65 (for his idea of a limitless first cause and was the author of the first book on nature)
- Right? (out of 20): 16 (sun is a huge mass and very far from Earth)
- Helpfully wrong? (out of 10): 9 (thought that the Earth was drum-shaped but this was helpful because his Earth floats free, leaving space for planets and stars to pass. Also had the idea that the Earth didn't move because it didn't have a good reason to do so which made others think about the causes of planetary motion
- Interesting death? (out of 10): 0 (not recorded)

Another man strides into the marketplace and interrupts. "No, no, no! You are both wrong. It is neither a boundless first cause or water, it is air that is the beginning of everything."

"Who's that?" asks Milton.

"Anaximenes, but you can call him Air Man," replies Zeno.

"Is that it? Have we heard all the theories? We've had the Water Man, Mr Boundless, and the Air Man. Can we vote for our favourite yet?" asks Milton.

"Not yet!" laughs Zeno. "There are still more to come. Ideas are cropping up thick and fast around here. They are all trying to identify the first cause, the really big story that is going to help us understand how nature works. Here's Pythagoras for instance. You might have heard of him."

"And what can we call him?" asks Milton.

Zeno smiles. "The Number One."

"People of Miletus, listen," calls Pythagoras. "Seriously, I mean listen really hard. Behind the movement of the moon, sun, and stars through the sky is a heavenly harmony if only our ears could hear it. And what is that music built on? I'll tell you – numbers! Mathematics lies behind everything; it is the first cause."

MEET THE SCIENTIST

PYTHAGORAS, THE NUMBER ONE

- Lived: c. 570–c. 495 BC
- Number of jobs: 4 (mathematician, musician, astronomer, and medic)
- Influence (out of 100): 90 (introduced maths into philosophy, started a vegetarian cult, and gave his name to a famous geometrical proof)
- Right? (out of 20): 16 (good at maths and said Earth wasn't stationary)
- Helpfully wrong? (out of 10): 5 (music of the spheres idea was wrong, but made lovely poetry)
- Interesting death? (out of 10): 4 (possibly starved to death)

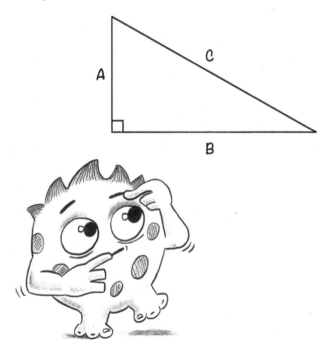

THE LEGEND OF PYTHAGORAS

Lots of zany tales involve Pythagoras, including one where he is the son of the god Apollo (his dad was actually a tradesman from the island of Samos, not far from Miletus). He was also said to shine with unnatural brightness and have a golden thigh (that must have been awkward).

Yet another man hurries on to the square. He can't keep still. "With respect, you are all wrong! Fire is the origin of everything. The world is in constant movement like the flickering of flames."

"That's Heraclitus," explains Zeno. "Naturally, we call him the Fire Man."

MEET THE SCIENTIST

HERACLITUS OF EPHESUS, FIRE MAN

- Lived: c. 535–c. 476 BC
- Number of jobs: 1 (philosopher)
- Influence (out of 100): 70 (idea that nature is in constant movement, fire is the basis of matter, and famous saying "no one ever steps in the same river twice")
- Right? (out of 20): 10 (nature does change constantly, but fire is not the basis of matter)
- Helpfully wrong? (out of 10): 3 (his idea of fire encouraged the four element theory which led to some scientific dead-ends, so largely unhelpful)
- Interesting death? (out of 10): 10 (asked to die stretched out in sunshine covered in cow dung)

"That must be it now," says Milton. His brain is spinning with all these conflicting opinions.

Harriet shakes her head. "Once the Greeks started thinking like this there was no stopping them. They were all curious about the first cause. Have a lie down in the shade."

Another man takes Heraclitus's place. "Everyone else is barking up the wrong tree!"

"That's Xenophanes," explains Zeno. "The God-Is-One man."

"I tell you that humans make gods in their own image – the Ethiopian god is black with a blunt nose, the Thracian, blue-eyed with red hair like them," cries Xenophanes. "But God does not have a human form. He is a single, motionless entity, at one with the universe! All things shiver at the impulse of His mind."

"So he's saying we're all part of some kind of God-mind?" asks Milton. "Like a thought?"

"Something like that," agrees Harriet.

Milton scratches his head. "I think I will take that lie-down you suggested."

He has just got settled when a dissenting voice strikes up at the far end of the marketplace. "Don't trust anything these people say!" the man shouts.

"That's Parmenides from Elea in southern Italy. We call him Mr Don't-Take-My-Word-for-It," says Zeno. "He thinks that any change is an illusion and that we have to doubt what our senses are telling us. But, hang on a moment, Empedocles has just edged him off his step."

"Parmenides is right in one way," says an earnest-looking man, "we can't rely on our senses. But that means we therefore have to pay very close attention to what we observe. I have concluded that there is no single cause but FOUR. Yes, four! We have fire, water, air, and earth all battling it out together under the forces that I will call love and strife."

Harriet nudges Milton awake. "Don't doze off now, Milton. Mr Four Elements has just introduced an idea that stuck around for two thousand years. And he has separated out matter and forces that work on it – that's really important for physics."

👍 (Mostly) Wrong Ideas Number 1 👎
The four elements

Scientific wrong ideas tend to have a long shelf life if the people who back them have a very impressive reputation. Empedocles's wrong idea that everything was made up of four elements – earth, air, water, and fire – stuck around so long because it was adopted by Aristotle, one of the next generation of great Greek scientists. Aristotle's ideas were taken up by the Islamic world and their scholars preserved and translated his works into Arabic. In turn these writings were translated into Latin for a western European audience in the thirteenth century.

And the lesson to learn? Even geniuses can get things wrong! Always go back to the evidence.

MEET THE SCIENTIST

EMPEDOCLES OF SICILY

- Lived: c. 490–c. 430 BC
- Number of jobs: 3 (philosopher, and – legend has it – magician and miraculous doctor who could stop old age, cure disease, and change the weather!)
- Influence (out of 100): 85 (introduced four elements idea)
- Right? (out of 20): 8 (separated matter from physical forces)
- Helpfully wrong? (out of 10): 2 (four elements idea was a problem!)
- Interesting death? (out of 10): 10 (said to have thrown himself into Mount Etna to prove he was immortal. The volcano burped back a smoking sandal, suggesting he wasn't)

And the finalists are...

Zeno lifts Milton onto his shoulder. "You mustn't miss this last speaker. Anaxagoras, also known as Mr Mind."

Harriet cranes her neck to see. "This is exciting! His big picture is the biggest of all and really changed the way people thought about nature!"

A stately man sweeps up to the top step. "People, how do we know anything? I'll tell you. It is because we use our intelligence to order our thoughts. That is true as well for the universe. A first intelligence orders everything. It follows then that we should use our brains and think about what we see so that we can come up with explanations."

"He's just invented scientific research," whispers Harriet. "It's a privilege to be here for this."

"Can I vote now?" asks Milton.

"Yes," says Harriet. "I've jotted them all down and you can pick your favourite.

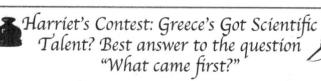

Harriet's Contest: Greece's Got Scientific Talent? Best answer to the question "What came first?"

- Lots of gods and goddesses on Olympus (how most Greeks thought)
- Water (Thales)
- Boundlessness (Anaximandros)
- Air (Anaximenes)
- Numbers (Pythagoras)
- Fire (Heraclitus)
- God-is-one (Xenophanes)
- Nothing changes (Parmenides)
- Four elements (Empedocles)
- The first mind (Anaxagoras)

"But which one is right?" asks Milton, not sure which to choose now he has to vote.

"The funny thing is that scientists are still asking variations of that same question today over two thousand years later," says Harriet. "And maybe the most important thing in this contest isn't their answers but the fact that they were curious enough to ask the question!"

Zeno and his paradoxes

Zeno takes all the scientists back to their homes in the time machine while Milton and Harriet think about the various ideas they have heard.

"Hang on a minute." Milton nudges Harriet. "Haven't you taken a bit of a risk involving our friend Zeno in all this? You might have changed the timeline."

Harriet smiles. "Don't worry I checked out our guide very carefully. He'll become a famous thinker himself. He grows up to follow Parmenides which means he doesn't trust his own senses and won't believe any of this has happened when we go. As time travel is full of paradoxes, I thought he'd like to see the time machine. Maybe we even helped because he will be famous for his paradoxes about space and time."

Milton still thinks Harriet has been a little reckless. "What's a paradox?"

"It's a statement that is absurd or seems to contradict itself but you can't show it to be wrong." Harriet sees Zeno returning and pats the bench beside her. "Ask him about my race with Achilles, the fastest man in Ancient Greece."

Milton curls up next to her. "Zeno, what's this about a race?"

Zeno grins and sits down to tell them his paradoxical story.

ZENO'S PARADOX: HARRIET THE TORTOISE VERSUS ACHILLES

The great runner Achilles challenges Harriet the tortoise to a hundred-metre race. Seeing she is somewhat slow, he offers to give her a ten-metre head start. The signal is given and the race begins. Yet no matter how hard Achilles runs, he never catches her. Each time he halves the distance between them, she has advanced a little way. Again, he halves the distance, but still she runs slowly forward and he still has to close that gap. Achilles will never be able to catch her as long as she keeps moving so the tortoise will win the race.

Milton scratches his nose. "But that's just silly! No disrespect, Harriet, to your athletic ability, which is no doubt amazing for a tortoise, but we all know that the fastest runner wins the race!"

Zeno strokes Milton's neck to soothe him. "Common sense says that, but mathematics doesn't. Logically there is no flaw in what I have just described. Want to hear another one? I've a great one about an arrow in flight."

"I'm not sure." Milton's brain is already buzzing.

"It's simple really. See this arrow." Zeno takes one of his arrows, strings it to the bow, and shoots it into the trunk of a nearby tree. He then draws the arrow's flight in the dust on the ground. "Now if I asked you where the arrow was a third of the way through it's journey, what would you say?"

"I'd say it was here." Milton points to a spot on the line with the tip of his tail.

"So it is definitely in that spot in the air then?" asks Zeno.

Milton fears a trap. "Well, yes."

"In that instant it is motionless in that spot?"

"I suppose, yes, in that tiny instant," says Milton, haltingly.

"And time is made up of tiny instants?"

"Yes."

"So each time we look where the arrow is, it is motionless in its place in the air for that instant?" Zeno asks.

"Um." Milton is no longer sure.

"There, you see, you clever cat! You've just proved that motion is impossible because objects are always without motion when measured."

Milton twitches his whiskers. "There's something fishy about this logic because things *do* move."

Zeno laughs so hard he has to sit down. "I know. Wonderfully paradoxical isn't it? I think that's going to give mathematicians a headache for centuries."

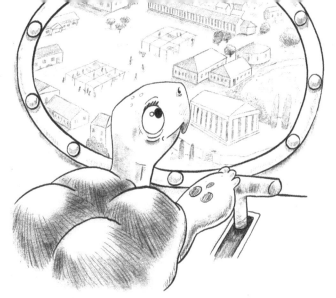

ATHENS TAKES TO THE STAGE

Harriet and Milton leave Zeno by the sea playing with his bow and arrows in the sunshine and get back into the time machine.

"Where are we going now?" asks Milton.

"I thought it was time we visited the ancient capital, Athens," says Harriet. "That is where the next stage in our scientific journey takes place."

Milton washes his paws. "What was wrong with Miletus? It was a nice spot with a port so everyone could come and go easily. We met lots of brilliant thinkers. Couldn't the philosophers have stayed around there and found a club or school to carry on their work?"

Harriet sets the destination on the control panel. "Unfortunately not. Historical events got in the way big time!"

Scatter Point Number 1:
Hit the road, Anax

In 499 BC Miletus was under the rule of a tyrant called Aristagoras. He wanted more power so told all the Greek-speaking cities of that part of the world to revolt against their Persian overlords. Bad idea! Persia was a big empire with masses of ships and armies so it wasn't a very equal fight. The revolt didn't go well and after six years of fighting, the Persians destroyed Miletus and many other cities as punishment for daring to resist them. For the story of science this meant that the clever thinkers from Miletus and surrounding cities were sent running for their lives. One of them, Anaxagoras, ended up as a refugee in Athens and so began a new chapter in scientific curiosity.

"So the war meant that people carried their ideas to other parts of Greece more quickly than they would otherwise have done?" says Milton.

"It looks that way," replies Harriet. "But that doesn't mean the thinkers received a warm welcome when they arrived. New ideas shake people up and can make them scared. It can lead to a clash between society and science – something we'll see again and again in our travels."

"Are we in danger now?" Milton is in two minds whether or not to leave the time machine now they've reached Athens.

Harriet nudges him towards the door. She knows he can be a bit of a scaredy-cat. "Not today as people have come to see a play and aren't going to notice us. I want to show you how the Athenians took to the new scientific ideas about the world."

"What did they do?" asks Milton. "Put up statues to the thinkers?"

"No, they laughed at them – and put one of them to death. Welcome to Athens – and yes," Harriet checks the clock on the wall of the time machine, "we're just in time for the show."

"What show is it?" Milton trots alongside Harriet as they enter an amphitheatre. The place is already packed with playgoers, sitting on the stone benches under a blue sky.

"On the stage today is a play called *The Clouds* by a famous writer, Aristophanes. It's a satire, which means it is making fun of a serious subject."

Milton scratches his ear. "Making fun? Why?"

"To reveal what is silly or weak about an idea or person."

Milton admires the theatre with its raked rows of seats and performance area far below. The actors are just coming on in their masks which have big features so they can be seen even by the people sitting right at the back. "This is exciting – and there's not a spare seat in the house!"

"The Greeks invented theatre and loved it," explains Harriet. "Everyone who can take a day off work is here. Athens is half empty."

"Wow," says Milton, looking around. "This is so cool: we're present not only at the start of science but theatre too!"

DEATH BY TORTOISE

Aeschylus was one of the most famous Greek playwrights, celebrated for his brilliant tragedies, but his own life had an equally dramatic conclusion. He is said to have been visiting Sicily in 458 BC and, while he was sunning himself outside the city of Gela, a passing eagle dropped a tortoise on his head, thinking his bald crown was a rock on which it could smash the shell and then eat its prey. Aeschylus died; the fate of the tortoise is not recorded.

Harriet checks the sky for passing eagles but fortunately it is clear. "They hold drama festivals like this one on religious holidays where different writers compete against each other. That's interesting for us because it tells us that, if Aristophanes is making fun of science in his play this year (423 BC), it means the ideas are well known enough for people to get the joke. They wouldn't laugh if they hadn't a clue what he was going on about, would they?"

Milton looks around eagerly. "I suppose not. So there's another vote?"

"That's right," says Harriet. "The Greeks are very serious about putting things to the public. You could say they invented the celebrity talent contest, but we won't hold it against them. Let's sit down and watch the performance. The show is about to start."

GreekEnders:
The Clouds

He's going to ruin us!

Son, it's time you turned your life around. I've put you down for the Thinkery.

Leave it out, Dad! I'm not hanging out with nerds!

Then I'll bloomin' well go myself.

And here's our latest discovery — how a gnat farts!

That's very... um... useful. Who came up with all this?

The End

Milton finds the play very funny. The scientists in the Thinkery were doing very silly experiments – measuring flea jumps, turning a scientist's instruments into a tool to steal cloaks, and observing the sun from a basket up in the air.

"How did the playwright get the idea that the philosophers were so foolish – and that it was all the fault of Socrates? Is he a famous scientist too?" he asks Harriet as they make their way out of the theatre with the rest of the audience.

"That's a little complicated. Let's wait in the shade while the crowds leave. I don't want to be stepped on." Harriet scuttles under a fig tree. Milton joins her. "I suppose there is a nugget of truth underneath the comedy. Aristophanes has two main targets – one is the science; the other is how new ways of thinking are upsetting the old rules of behaviour."

"So Socrates is to blame for all that?" asks Milton.

"No – and that's the odd thing. He paid the price but wasn't really responsible for either. All he did was ask awkward questions. He made people think and stirred their curiosity about the world we can see and measure. I think I need to tell you a little more so you can understand. Let's look at the so-called odd experiments first. That all starts with a meteorite."

"Me-Ooow! Sounds exciting."

50

"Almost too exciting for the farmers of Thrace, a region north-east of Athens," explains Harriet. "In 467 BC the local people got a shock when a meteorite fell during daylight and crashed in a field. It was a brown rock the size of a cart and many people went to have a look at it. The meteorite hit the spot for Anaxagoras too because he had a theory that the stars are made of stone – radical thinking for the time."

WANTED: ANAXAGORAS, THE REVOLUTIONARY SCIENTIST

This man, also known by his nickname Mr First Mind, is believed to be on the loose in Athens. He passes on to his gang of thinkers his outrageous ideas as to how the universe works.

He is wanted for the following revolutionary theories:

• There is one first mind that orders the universe.

• The objects we see in the heavens are made of stone.

• The sun is a ball of fire, bigger than Greece.

• The moon only shines because it reflects light.

• The moon has valleys like Earth.

• Solar eclipses are caused by the moon passing over the face of the sun.

• His ideas are DANGEROUS and go against everything we know. He should be approached with caution.

Signed THE CITIZENS OF ATHENS

"They may not have wanted his ideas," continues Harriet, "but we know now that much of this is right."

"Not the theory about the sun," says Milton. "My master Schrödinger told me that the sun is actually 109 times bigger and you can fit well over a million Earths inside it."

Harriet nods. "Yes, but Anaxagoras got the idea that the sun was much bigger than anyone had thought before. Imagine, though, if you were a normal Greek person who believed Zeus and Helios were running the show in the sky and the sun was the size of a chariot. You would think this was all extraordinary "up in the air" thinking. You might even think it a threat to your gods as it changes how you think about the sky and the sun."

Milton's whiskers tremble a little. "You've got me worried now. What happened to clever Mr First Mind?"

"Anaxagoras realized that he wasn't very popular so he went into exile to a little place called Lampsacus where the people liked him," Harriet explains. "When he died a few years later, they built an altar to his ideas of Mind and Truth in his memory."

The crowd has gone so Milton leads the way back to the time machine. "Harriet, I was wondering: is this the first time people's desire to protect their belief in their gods clashes with science?"

"It might be – and it won't be the last. People in Athens thought their gods needed defending from new ideas about the universe and didn't stop to wonder if the theories might be true. Not everyone is happy with where curiosity takes them."

"So that was the science the play was mocking," says Milton. "But what about the new ways of thinking?"

Harriet smiles. "The new thinking came out of the new public sport."

"What was that?" asks Milton. "Football? Chess? Tiddlywinks?

"No, debating."

Milton looks unconvinced. "Debating!"

"You've seen that Athens invented elections," says Harriet. "That meant they also invented politicians and election campaigns."

Milton sniffs. "Was that a good idea?"

"Having a vote is better than not having one."

"True," says Milton.

"The candidates in Athenian elections had to speak to ordinary men and use arguments to win them over," explains Harriet. "In other words, they learned the gift of the gab. Schools were set up to teach debating as number one on the curriculum. And one of the best debate teams in Athens were called the Sophists."

"That Protagoras chap makes a very difficult guest," says Milton.

"That's because he sees no firm basis for belief," says Harriet. "He realized that humans in different places have different views on important questions of right and wrong. He said 'Man is the measure of all things' meaning it is only humans who make laws or beliefs so how can you say one is more right than another?"

Milton tries to puzzle this out. "So if I steal your lettuce..."

"Hey!"

"Not hay, you eat lettuce," laughs Milton. "And it's only an example – I'm not really going to do it."

Harriet frowns. "Oh all right then. Carry on."

"If I steal your lettuce because I say in my view it's fine to take it from you, then your opinion doesn't matter?" says Milton.

Harriet ducks into her shell and is relieved to find her store of lettuce is safe. "That's where the Sophist's philosophy leads if some shared values can't be agreed." She pops her head out again. "And can you see now – that's what Aristophanes said the son in *The Clouds* learned in the Thinkery – ways to excuse men behaving badly!"

Milton nods. "I get that now. You have two main threats to society: theories that edge out the actions of gods and ideas that make behaviour a free-for-all. A society might collapse if it went that way."

"Exactly," says Harriet, "which is why Athens punished its thinkers: it got scared."

SOCRATES: DOCTOR WHY?

One of the most famous casualties of this battle between curiosity and society is a Greek thinker called Socrates (c. 470–399 BC). Before becoming known for his philosophy, he was both a stonemason and a soldier, serving with distinction in the Peloponnesian war with neighbouring Sparta. He was a hoplite; that meant he was skilled wielding a spear and shield. He was an action man before he became known as a thinking man.

Socrates arrived back in Athens with a new way of thinking: question everything to get at the true reasons for action. This can be used on scientific theories about how the world works as well as why humans act as we do. In this, he was influenced by Anaxagoras's idea of the First Mind which orders the world but Socrates was disappointed that Anaxagoras stopped in the physical realm. He wanted people to ask big "why" questions so they could see how the smaller ones about the physical world fitted into the picture. Socrates turned from questioning events like eclipses of the sun to investigating morality and ethics – in other words the reasons behind the things people do.

Enter Pythia – the great snake priestess – to the drama of Socrates's life. The Greeks set great store by the pronouncements of oracles who were special priests or priestesses serving the gods in temples around Greece. The most important of these was Pythia, the priestess at the Temple of Apollo in Delphi, and the most powerful woman in the ancient world.

She gave a prophecy that Socrates was the wisest man alive. This disturbed Socrates because he knew he knew nothing.

He went around Athens questioning all those said to be the cleverest in their fields – politicians, writers, artists. He concluded that they also knew nothing but he had the edge because, unlike them, he was aware of his ignorance.

I know that I know nothing – therefore I'm the cleverest!

That was the foundation of his thought: admitting your ignorance is the beginning of wisdom. The danger to Athenian society was that sceptical minds like the Sophists could turn this to mean that there is no possibility of any real kind of knowledge. Socrates himself believed his ignorant wisdom was in service to a First Mind, or a good and wise God. He thought there was a moral order to the universe that could be discovered by deep questioning.

Unfortunately, Socrates had made quite a few enemies with his pesky habit of questioning everything. He had also dared to suggest that justice and goodness should come before the interests of the state. He had even praised their enemy, Sparta. Having annoyed the people in power, he was put on trial for corrupting the minds of the Athenian youth and for not believing in the gods of the state – a slanted version of the truth which echoed how Aristophanes had portrayed him in *The*

Clouds. Socrates was found guilty and sentenced to drink a cup of hemlock, a deadly poison. He had the chance to flee but decided that he did not fear death. He had placed himself under Athenian justice by living there so would accept the verdict. He died heroically from the feet up (the effect of the poison numbs you from the toes to the head) surrounded by his admirers. He tried to make the point in his death that reasoning your way to the truth was a religious duty and worth a sacrifice.

"That doesn't seem fair," says Milton. "Killing him when all he did was ask questions."

"Curiosity is a dangerous thing – and Socrates knew that," replies Harriet.

"So do cats!"

"But you have nine lives; he only had one." Harriet ushers Milton back inside the time machine.

"So what happened next?" asks Milton.

"For a few years following his death, things looked bleak in Athens for his followers," explained Harriet. "While they go off to find safer places to carry on their questioning, we are going to go forward in time to the next stage on our curious quest."

AND THE ACADEMY AWARD GOES TO...

Scatter Point Number 2:
Plato on his gap years

The death of Socrates showed that Athens had become a dangerous place to be a thinker. His admirers scattered. The most famous among these was Plato. He fled to Italy where a group of Pythagoras's disciples had a community at Tarentum. It was led by a mathematical wizard, Archytas, who also managed to be a popular leader.

ARCHYTAS, THE SUPER KING

- Lived: c. 428–c. 347 BC
- Number of jobs: 5 (brilliant general, philosopher, inventor, musician, and political leader)
- Influence (out of 100): 70 (gave shelter to Plato, described chromatic musical scale, invented mathematical mechanics, promoted maths as the basis of scientific truths)
- Right? (out of 20): 15 (doubling of cube solution in maths, invented first steam-powered machine called The Pigeon)
- Helpfully wrong? (out of 10): 1 (mostly right)
- Interesting death? (out of 10): 7 (died in a shipwreck)

Milton gets out of the time machine and finds they are still in Athens. "Hey, what are we doing back here? I thought you said it wasn't safe?"

Harriet ambles past him, completely untroubled. "Don't get your tail in a twist, Milton. We've come forward in time to 387 BC. It is OK to be a thinker again."

"So where are we going? To see another play?" asks Milton eagerly.

"No, we're going to school."

"School?" Milton's whiskers droop in disappointment.

"We are paying a call on the original Academy," explains Harriet. "Actually, it is more like a club than a school. Set in an olive grove sacred to Athena, the goddess of wisdom, it lies outside the city walls."

Milton frowns. "A school in the garden? What do they do there? Grow vegetables?"

"No, talk," says Harriet.

"Talk?"

"It is what the Ancient Greeks do best, remember? On his return from his gap years with Archytas and travelling around the Mediterranean, Plato created the Academy as a place for philosophical discussion and debate," Harriet tells him. "The members even include two women – Axiothea and Lasthenia – which is almost unheard of in ancient times as women aren't usually allowed to study."

"What do they talk about?" Milton asks.

Harriet stops underneath the door to the Academy. "They start with geometry."

Milton reads the sign and his whiskers droop further. "Uh-oh. They'll never let me in."

"Can you do geometry, Harriet?" Milton asks.

Harriet blushes. "I have to admit that it's not my strong point. I always used to sleep inside my shell during maths lessons in the Darwin nursery. I think we're going to need some help."

TRY THIS AT HOME: CAN YOU HELP HARRIET AND MILTON ENTER THE ACADEMY?

Solve the following geometrical puzzle to earn them entry into Plato's garden. Draw lines to divide this picture into four identical sections. See the answer at the back of the book!

"I'm relieved we got past that with some help," says Milton. "Let's go and find this Plato person and see what he has to add to science."

"I think you'll find him a curious person. For one, he wrote a lot. His writings are how we know about Socrates because Socrates didn't write his ideas down. But Plato had his own theories too. He was another person who asked big questions before he asked specific questions about the natural world."

Milton and Harriet find Plato walking with students along the shady paths of the Academy.

"Excuse me, Mr Plato," pipes up Milton, "but can you explain to me what you think lies behind the universe. Other people have suggested water, fire, the First Mind and so on. What do you think?"

"A very good question, Mr Cat," says Plato. "I follow in the footsteps of Pythagoras and think numbers lie behind everything because in them we get as close as possible to the ultimate reality."

"Me-ow, ultimate reality – that sounds cool," mews Milton. "But, um, what does that mean?"

"Let us sit for a moment and I'll explain."

Plato's class settle around him. One student takes Milton onto her lap while another feeds fresh leaves to Harriet.

"Imagine we are all in a cave. The ultimate reality is behind us outside the cave but we are sitting facing the wall where only the flickering shadows of what is real appear. We learn from those shadows to guess at what the ultimate forms might be without ever seeing them in their purest shape.

"Take Mr Cat here. He is a very fine cat, no doubt, but you've also seen finer ones and dirtier ones, ones with short hair, ones with long hair, a cat with three legs, and maybe one with no tail. All are different, yet they all share in common their catness and you have no trouble calling them all 'cat'. That is because we recognize the flickering shadow of the pure cat form in these imperfect creatures."

"Steady on," mutters Milton, not too keen on this talk of imperfection.

Plato continues, "By contrast to things by which we are surrounded like cats, dogs, people, tables, and all the other objects that we see daily, numbers are closest to the form for which they stand. Numbers suggest the harmony and order underlying both the physical universe and moral truths."

"What does he mean?" Milton whispers to Harriet.

Harriet smiles. "That numbers rule, OK?"

"Now, my young disciples, I have a challenge for you," continues Plato. "If the universe is governed by heavenly harmony, how can the movement of the stars and planets be explained? What is the secret order behind what appear to be disorderly motions? That's your homework."

The students disperse to think and talk some more about the challenge Plato has set them. Plato lies on his back and goes to sleep in the sunshine.

"Why does he think the movement of the stars is disorderly?" whispers Milton, not wanting to wake the great thinker.

"Because at this time their model of the universe is wrong," Harriet whispers back. "They put the Earth at the centre and they don't realize it travels around the sun and that the sun itself is at the centre of one universe in a much larger galaxy that continues to expand. If you don't know any of that, you have to account for planets that seem to wander around the skies without any predictable movements."

Milton frowns. "Shall we tell him?"

"Milton!"

"But you told Zeno about the time machine," Milton protests.

"That was different," says Harriet.

"Isn't."

"Is."

"Why?" asks Milton, sulkily.

"For one," says Harriet, "because Plato is much more influential and people have to find these things out for themselves when they are ready."

Milton settles down next to Plato with a grumble but decides not to undermine the historical timeline.

A shabbily dressed student comes running back with his answer.

"Sir, sir, I think I've cracked it!"

Harriet nudges Milton. "Wake up; you're about to meet someone very interesting. This young man is extraordinary."

Milton yawns. "He looks like he's been sleeping under a hedge for a month."

"Not a hedge, a boat," says Harriet. "He is so poor, he walks in daily to hear Plato's lectures and returns each night to sleep in the boat that brought him to Athens. That's dedication!"

Hearing his favourite pupil approaching, Plato sits up, dislodging the daisy chain that Harriet has been weaving into his beard. "What's that, Eudoxos?"

"I think I've solved the question of planetary motion. Here!" The young student shows Plato his first attempt to explain the heavens by a mathematical order.

👍 (Mostly) Wrong Ideas Number 2 👎

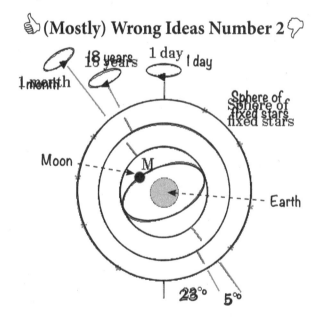

"That's not right," hisses Milton. "He's got planets going backwards and forwards like spaghetti on a plate."

"Sssh," says Harriet, trying to keep Milton from interfering while Plato congratulates his pupil. "It's a very helpful kind of wrong."

"You're kidding me?"

"I'm not," says Harriet. "It is a starting point for other stargazers as it confirms that planets can move in a way predicted by mathematics. It suggests a universe formed to a rational design – one that you can study. Plato goes on to say that astronomy has been leading thinkers towards atheism; discovering an underlying order allows them to now see a divine craftsman behind creation. Science and religion can travel happily in each other's slipstream for a time."

A SURPRISING NOTE ON PLATO

His birth name was Aristocles but he was given the nickname Plato because he was "broad" (the meaning in Greek) – we don't know if that refers to his chest measurement or his interests. He also wore an earring in his youth. See if your teacher knows that!

Class is dismissed for the day. As Eudoxos goes off to his boat to sleep, Harriet and Milton return to the time machine.

"Where next?" asks Milton.

Harriet sets the controls. "Not far. We're going forward a few years to visit the next big school in Athens. It was set up by another student of Plato, a man Plato called 'the Brain.'"

Milton looks intrigued. "Who is he?"

"Aristotle. You could argue he was the most important Greek scientist of them all."

DOCTOR, DOCTOR...

ALCMAEON

Before Harriet and Milton drop in on Aristotle, we should take a look at another area of science. The Greeks were also pioneers in the field of medicine. Alcmaeon (c. 510 BC) of Croton in southern Italy led the way. Said to be a student of Pythagoras, he took a different route from his teacher, concentrating on human health. He was the first to suggest that illness was the result of an imbalance in the humours (which identified that to be ill something was wrong *inside* the patient – an important advance). He also linked illness to diet, lifestyle, and environment – a theory with which a modern doctor would agree.

One huge advance for understanding how our bodies work was that he was the first to realize that the brain was the seat of understanding.

I wonder...?

Medicine heads in the right direction

HIPPOCRATES

Alcmaeon was followed by Hippocrates (c. 460 BC) from the Greek island of Kos. He is remembered today as doctors still take the Hippocratic oath on entering the profession by which they swear to do no harm to the patient and try to prevent disease as prevention is better than cure – all ideas first suggested in Hippocrates's writings. As for his contribution to science, Hippocrates established the idea that illness had a physical cause rather than being a punishment from the gods. This allowed doctors to look for physical cures.

Less helpfully, he also developed the idea of the four humours that said the human body contained black bile, yellow bile, phlegm, and blood. These corresponded to four temperaments: melancholy, quick-tempered, peaceful, and optimistic.

Melancholy

Quick-tempered

Peaceful

Optimistic

He believed that illness resulted from an imbalance between them. That is why for many centuries many doctors used such practices as bleeding a patient: they thought they were restoring balance. This idea stayed around for over two thousand years, only fading in the Victorian era.

HAVE YOU MET
THE BRAIN?

The time machine makes the short hop to Aristotle's Athens. Harriet emerges first, followed by Milton.

"When are we?" he asks.

"In 335 BC."

"Is it safe to be a thinker now?" Milton sniffs the air.

"For a time," says Harriet, "until the Romans attack in 86 BC."

Milton relaxes. "Good, we've got a breathing space of a few hundred years."

Harriet shakes her head. "Not if you're one of Aristotle's pupils. His school, the Lyceum, only lasts 12 years under him until he finds himself on the wrong side of history."

"That seems to happen to the Ancient Greeks a lot," Milton says. "So what's Aristotle's school like in this year?"

"There were already sports grounds and meeting places on the site," explains Harriet, "but Aristotle adds a library and a collection of creatures and botanical specimens from all over the known world."

"A school with a zoo? That's brilliant!" claims Milton.

Harriet smiles. "The animals were sent to him by a grateful past pupil."

"That's a bit more than an apple for your favourite teacher. I guess that the student must have travelled quite a bit?" says Milton.

Harriet nods. "I'll say. He was called Alexander the Great. He came from the small Greek state of Macedon and he would conquer the known world all the way to India."

"That's a lot of botanical specimens."

"You're right. It can also be called a huge data collection which Aristotle tried to explain and classify. This is why some say that Aristotle invented the science of biology," explains Harriet.

They enter the garden of the Lyceum to find Aristotle teaching. He does this while striding at quite a speed along the paths of the gardens. Harriet is soon out of breath and fears she is missing all the exciting bits. She pulls at the sandal of the nearest student.

"Would you mind giving me a lift?"

The student bends down. "Sir, sir, I have another tortoise specimen for you. Do you want to dissect it?"

Harriet disappears into her shell very quickly.

Aristotle strokes his beard and winks at Milton, who stands ready to defend Harriet with teeth and claws if necessary. "Stand down, brave cat. There is no need to spring into action as I've already explored tortoise anatomy and written about it in my scrolls. Leave her be. She can listen if she wants."

The student picks up Harriet but she decides it is safer to listen from inside her shell.

"All men by nature desire to know," continues Aristotle. "It is through our wonder at the world that we originally began to ask questions. When we are curious about small matters, step by step we raise questions about great ones."

"So, sir, what is the origin of these things?" asks Milton, remembering the debate he heard at Miletus.

"The final cause. The unmoved mover. God, the eternal most good," says Aristotle. "If we think about these matters we are fulfilling our purpose as the end of human life is to study."

After listening for an hour to Aristotle's lecture, hearing him hop from subject to subject, Milton and Harriet get tired and take a rest in his library.

"That's all a bit too much to take in at one sitting. Let's see if the library can show us where Aristotle's curiosity about big questions takes him," suggests Milton.

"That'll keep us busy for years: there is nothing that doesn't interest him when it comes to the things we can see," sighs Harriet, looking at the hundreds of scrolls in their niches. She dips inside her shell and returns with a piece of paper. "Here: I've written him a school report to summarise his achievements."

ARISTOTLE

....

SCHOOL REPORT

*Metaphysics: Grade A**

Aristotle is a clever student who takes his master's (Plato's) ideas on forms and suggests that rather than these ideals living out there "beyond the cave", they exist in things in the shape of four causes: a thing's material (what it is made of), formal (how it is formed), efficient (what causes it to change), and final cause (what purpose it has).

Sounds tricky? It makes more sense when applied. Take a dining table. Its material cause is wood; its formal the design of the carpenter; its efficient the work the carpenter did to make it; and its final cause is so we can eat dinner off it.

Biology: Grade B++

Aristotle is an eager pupil, a delight to teach, who collects specimens from across the world and on his own doorstep. He is the first to try to classify and order as he believes that the world has a purpose and underlying order. He shows excellent initiative in producing reference scrolls with diagrams to pass on knowledge and has been claimed as the founder of biology (reward trip earned).

Unfortunately, occasional errors creep into his work which he passes on to later generations and I won't mention what he did to some tortoises.

Physics: Grade C-

Aristotle tries hard, and remains an asset in the classroom for his enthusiasm for the subject, but sadly he hasn't yet realized the value of experimentation and repeatable observations that will become scientific method in later times. I have marked him perhaps a little harshly but this is because, despite his undoubted brilliance as a scholar, he sends physics off track with three of his main ideas.

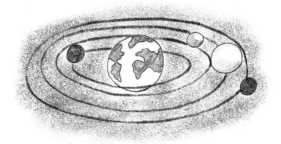

One: his model of the universe puts Earth at the centre with the planets and fixed stars circling in separate spheres. This idea remains set in people's minds for a thousand years until the Renaissance – and this is despite other more correct theories being available.

Air

Aether

Fire

Earth

Water

Two: he adopts Empedocles's idea of the four elements and adds a fifth, Aether, the stuff that fills the heavenly spheres and is not subject to change. He does this with no experimental proof but rather, I believe, because he finds it a nice idea and fits his model of the universe. He should rather spend his time making his model fit what he can observe.

Three: some of his ideas about motion are just wrong. He believes that a heavier object will fall faster than a lighter one. He also thinks that as an arrow moves through air, the air makes way, rushes around to fill the gap where it was, and so "pushes" the arrow forward. Amazingly, this odd idea catches on and won't be refuted for centuries.

Logic: Grade A*

Aristotle aces this one as he invents the subject. At its heart is his use of something called a syllogism as a way of organising thought. It is easier to see in practice than describe. It goes through three stages. Here is an example:

Humans are mortal

Aristotle is a human

Aristotle is mortal

That's a simple example but it can be used to test all sorts of ideas to see if the logical steps are being taken. So take this false example:

Dangerous dogs have big teeth

Your dog has big teeth

Your dog is dangerous

A clever thinker will see that an error has crept in. Having big teeth doesn't make a dog dangerous and there are friendly dogs with big teeth that pose no risk. So by organising thought in this way, you can see where the error in logic lies.

Ethics: Grade A

Aristotle applies his idea of the four causes to humans and says that the final cause of a person is to aim for excellence and well-being, which includes doing good.

He takes ethics from a theory to being a practical goal of good living.

Politics and government: Grade A

He has an advanced concept of the "city state" existing like an organism for the benefit of its parts; allowing citizens, not only safety, justice, and a chance to make a living, but to live a good life and perform beautiful deeds.

Other subjects (rhetoric, poetry, theatre criticism, music etc): Grade A

Aristotle shows his artistic side here as he blazes the way for other thinkers in these areas too, writing on the main forms of theatre of his day (tragedy and comedy, though his work on comedy is lost) and music. Many later writers copied and developed his ideas. He also liked collecting riddles and fables, such as those by Aesop.

Conclusion

Aristotle is the most impressive student I've met in Ancient Greece and even his mistakes are but the result of an active mind wanting to know everything. I'm sure he will go far if he only leaves tortoises alone.

Signed

Harriet the Tortoise

ARISTOTLE AND THE SNORING DOLPHINS

While some of Aristotle's ideas in physics may not have been well observed, he made some surprising discoveries in zoology that can only have been based on first-hand accounts, either from what he observed or what those who knew the animals told him. Three in particular have only been confirmed by biologists who came along centuries later.

• Daddy catfish: Aristotle claimed that catfish in his part of the Mediterranean left the protection of eggs and fry to the male fish. This went against expectations that it would be the mothers who would stay to look after the young. This was found to be true but not until scientists in the nineteenth century took a closer look at the breed in his local river.

• Mermaid purses: Have you ever been to a beach and seen black pods washed up on the shore? These have been given the name "mermaid purses" because they are just the right size in which to keep a comb and little shell or two. Aristotle rightly suggested they were the discarded outer coating of fish eggs. He said they came from dogfish and now we know that that is true and that other species also produce them, such as sharks.

• Snoring dolphins: In what was possibly the first live mark and recapture programme for scientific purposes, Aristotle investigated the noises made by dolphins. He suggested that they snore during sleep. Modern scientists have found that while dolphins don't snore in the way a human does, they do make sounds during sleep so Aristotle wasn't far off the mark.

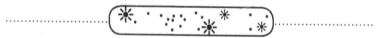

Scatter Point Number 3:
Problems with a past pupil

"Very impressive. But you said, Harriet, that Aristotle ended up on the wrong side of history. So what happened?" asks Milton, handing the report back to Harriet.

"Remember the specimen-collecting student who conquered the world?" she asks.

"Alexander the Great?"

Harriet nods. "Yes. Alexander was originally from a little state called Macedon. First his father, then Alexander led their armies successfully, broke the power of Persia, and conquered a huge empire. He didn't live long to enjoy his conquests. He died aged only 32 in Babylon in 322 BC, possibly poisoned, though it may have just been a fever."

"Me-owch! Sounds like a case for the police!"

"Unfortunately, they didn't have detectives or forensic science then so the exact cause of death remains a mystery," explains

Harriet. "It's true, though, that Alexander made a lot of enemies."

Milton scratches his ear. "Conquering the world does that to a person."

"Quite. Aristotle was Alexander's tutor until he was 16 so was known as one of his team. On news of Alexander's death, Athens rose against Macedon and Aristotle became a marked man. He fled and died in exile."

"So with Aristotle fled, did that mean school was out?" Milton's whiskers prick up in hope.

Harriet smiles and shakes her head. "No, just that the Lyceum had to find a new headteacher. And before you get the idea this school was the only one in town, I thought before we finally leave Athens we'd pay a quick visit to the two other places that you can go to if you are an Athenian youth – places that didn't encourage the study of science. They are a kind of footnote to the Lyceum."

"So where are they?" asks Milton.

"The first one is right in the city centre, in the Painted Porch," replies Harriet. "This is a colonnade that provided shelter for those who wanted to teach there. In fact the porch gave the school its name. The Greek for porch is "stoa" and they became known as the Stoics."

"I think I've heard of them. Aren't they known for suffering in silence?"

"In a way." Harriet nudges Milton to the edge of the crowd sitting around a man in the porch. "That's Zeno."

"Our Zeno with the paradoxes?" asks Milton.

"No, a later one. This is Zeno of Citium. His ideas became a popular way of thinking in the ancient world for centuries."

Harriet's Footnote Number 1: The danger of the stubbed toe

Zeno of Cilium (c. 334 BC) is said to have washed up in Athens after surviving a shipwreck. He wandered into a bookshop (obviously anyone's first port of call after a brush with death) and found the writings of Socrates. Inspired by these, he set up his own school, saying that happiness was to be found in living a life of virtue. He claimed that studying nature was beyond the realm of philosophy which should only concern itself with the mind.

He is said to have met his death in 262 BC by stubbing his toe. In response he held his breath and died. An odd footnote to an influential life!

"When you said 'footnote', you weren't joking!" says Milton. "So what about the other school?"

"That one takes place in a garden. The school of the Epicureans."

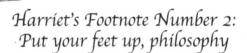

Harriet's Footnote Number 2: Put your feet up, philosophy

This school was founded by a Greek called Epicurus (341–270 BC). His philosophy starts with a scientific theory. There was a thinker called Democritus (c. 460 BC) who was one of the first to suggest that all things were made of atoms. He went on to say that natural processes could be explained without reference to the gods. Epicurus took this to mean that the soul was also atomic; there was no need to fear judgement in an afterlife because it did not exist in a material world. In the light of that humans should live to please themselves and aim to be at peace.

Some say that his scepticism that nothing can be believed contributed to the development of scientific thinking. On the other hand, he also seemed to have thought that research is futile as it did not contribute to peace of mind.

So living without fear of divine punishment, in a universe that Epicurus thought was eternal and the result of the movement of atoms, it was time for philosophy to put its feet up in the garden and chill. If you lose interest in the big questions, maybe you soon lose interest in the material world too.

SCIENCE ON THE NILE

Milton watches out of the porthole of the time machine as Athens vanishes into the mists of time. Harriet sets a course for the next destination.

"So what happens in science after Aristotle had to run away?" Milton asks.

"The centre of scientific thought moves to Africa. To Egypt." Harriet points to the map she drew for him at the beginning of the adventure. "At the exit of the Nile into the Mediterranean is one of the most amazing cities in the ancient world: Alexandria."

"Is that anything to do with Alexander the Great?"

"Yes, well done!" Harriet says.

Milton makes a face. "The name is a bit of a clue, Harriet. It wasn't that clever of me."

"Still, it shows you are keeping up," says Harriet, smiling. "Alexander founded it shortly before he died. What happened next was that his vast empire was divided up between his generals, because it was too big for one person to rule. Alexandria and Egypt fell to Ptolemy I. He was the one who really kick-started the process of making it into the centre of learning by bringing top scholars to his city and giving them money to buy books."

HELLENISTIC PERIOD: CURIOUS DEFINITIONS

This has nothing to do with anyone called Helen. This term is taken from the German word for Ancient Greece (hellenistisch). The Greeks themselves had no idea that this was what they were living through as the name came much later. For us it means the time from the death of Alexander to when Rome takes over this part of the world in 31 BC.

Helen

German academic

"Wasn't one of the Wonders of the World there?" muses Milton.

"The lighthouse, which was built in the harbour around this time and was one of the tallest man-made structures in the world for centuries," Harriet explains. "But that's only the start of the famous places in the city. The lighthouse survived for centuries, finally being ruined by an earthquake in the fourteenth century. It was the third longest surviving of the Seven Wonders."

"I know the last one standing," Milton says, looking pleased with himself. "The Great Pyramid of Giza."

"That's right! That can still be found many miles up the Nile from Alexandria," says Harriet. "And in case you are curious, the final one to be destroyed was the Mausoleum of Halicarnassus, which was also destroyed by an earthquake in the fifteenth century."

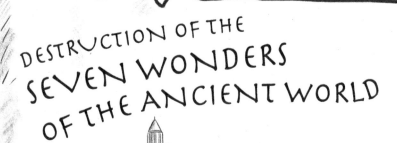

DESTRUCTION OF THE
SEVEN WONDERS
OF THE ANCIENT WORLD

**LIGHTHOUSE OF
ALEXANDRIA
(EARTHQUAKE)**

**MAUSOLEUM OF
HALICARNASSUS
(EARTHQUAKE)**

**HANGING GARDENS
OF BABYLON
(FATE UNKNOWN)**

THE COLOSSUS OF
RHODES
(EARTHQUAKE)

TEMPLE OF ARTEMIS
(SACKED BY GOTHS)

STATUE OF ZEUS
(FATE UNKNOWN)

THE GREAT
PYRAMID OF GIZA
(STILL STANDING!)

"It's a good job that they built the pyramid to withstand earthquakes and raiders."

"Egyptian builders were very clever. Here in Alexandria they also built the world's most famous library, as well as a museum and lecture halls."

Landing on the top of the lighthouse, still so brand new that the builders are only just removing the scaffolding, our two explorers get out of the time machine for the best view of the city. They look across the bay to the Royal Quarter, the museum and library, grand places built in the Greek style they first saw in Athens. The pale stone of the buildings is almost blinding to gaze upon in the hot sunshine.

"I could do with going somewhere shady," says Milton.

"Let's go into the city and see what we can find. And then I think we should head to the library."

UNLIKELY HEROES: ENTER THE LIBRARIANS!

The ancient world throws up some unexpected superheroes. Three of these served as chief librarians in Alexandria. The first of these is Dimitrios of Phaleron. One of the scholarly exiles from Athens after the death of Alexander, he fell on his feet when he was given the budget by Ptolemy I to collect "all the books in the world" which he pretty well managed to do. The library collection became the centrepiece of knowledge that allowed other scholars to study and make their scientific advances. He held the post until 284 BC.

Another noted library hero was one of his successors, Callimachus of Cyrene (c. 310–240 BC), who classified the 120,000 books in the collection according to author and subject – amazingly this was the first time anyone had thought to do that.

BEFORE CALLIMACHUS

I want the scroll about animals. I think it's kind of brown and about this big...

AFTER CALLIMACHUS

History of Animals by Aristotle? Here it is.

The third hero was called Eratosthenes (276–194 BC), librarian under Ptolemy II. He had the misfortune to be second best in so many fields that he was nicknamed Beta (the second letter in the Greek alphabet) – a little like being known as Robin to Batman. For example, in astronomy he was runner-up to Aristarchus of Samos (c. 310–230 BC) who is famous for suggesting that the sun was the centre of the solar system – a truth that was not widely accepted until some eighteen centuries later. Eratosthenes was no joker though, because he calculated to an impressive degree of accuracy the circumference of the Earth (the distance around the planet). He did this by comparing at the same time the angle of shadows at noon in Alexandria and in Syene, a place directly to the south. From the difference in the angles he could calculate that the two places were a fiftieth of the circumference. He already knew how far Alexandria and Syene were so could do a simple multiplication to come up with the total. He got it right to within about 16 per cent of the generally accepted figure nowadays. So if anyone tells you that in those days people thought the Earth was flat…!

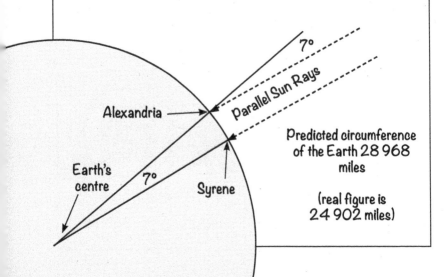

7°

Parallel Sun Rays

Alexandria

Predicted circumference of the Earth 28 968 miles

(real figure is 24 902 miles)

Earth's centre

7°

Syrene

Harriet and Milton arrive in Alexandria and take a tour of the city, keeping to the shady side of the streets. Milton is impressed by the number of cat statues and the respectful treatment he is shown by the locals.

"Here's another place that knows how to treat cats!" he tells Harriet. He winds around the ankles of a market stallholder.

"Hello, my lovely," the stallholder says, offering him a piece of dried fish.

"Is it just me, or are all cats special here?" Milton asks hopefully.

The woman chuckles. "All, because you are sacred to the goddess Bastet. If you stick around long enough, we'll even mummify you when you die and take you to her temple in Bast."

"Oh, er, no thanks. Appreciate the thought and everything." Milton hurries on. "They mummify cats here!" he squeaks to Harriet.

"Oh yes," nods Harriet. "You can see lots of them in museums in our time. It was quite a curious tradition."

"Did they mummify tortoises?

"Not that I'm aware." Harriet ambles along while Milton scurries after her, casting fearful looks over his shoulder. "I'm sure you're perfectly safe."

"Safe? It's not you they are threatening to pull your brains out through your nostrils, embalm them in herbs, and wrap them in bandages!"

"They'll give you mummified mice and milk for the afterlife," Harriet informs him.

"You aren't making me feel better!"

Harriet decides it is time to stop teasing Milton. "Don't worry, nothing will happen to you. They'll wait until you die a natural death before they do that."

"Then we'd better not hang around here too long."

They enter the library and find a young student poring over the works of a mathematician called Euclid. Harriet nudges Milton.

"See that library scroll? Euclid was one of the most important thinkers to come out of Alexandria even though very little is known about his life. He has been called the Father of Geometry and his book stayed as the main school text book for mathematics until the nineteenth century."

"Not more mathematics," groans Milton.

"Don't worry. We will get this student to help us. His name is Archimedes and he becomes as famous as Euclid once he graduates from Alexandria."

Harriet taps the young student on the toe. "Excuse me?"

The student looks down at the two hopeful animals. "Oh, hello." He bows low to Milton. "How can I help?"

"Can you explain what you are reading?" asks Harriet. "Neither my friend nor I are good at maths."

Archimedes lifts Harriet onto his desk. Milton jumps onto his lap. "Be my guest. Take a look at my notes."

How many sacks are they each carrying?

"That doesn't sound too bad," agrees Harriet, having worked out the answer in her head.

"Euclid starts with things that seem simple," says Archimedes. "We call them axioms – a starting point like 'It is possible to draw a straight line between any two points' – and goes from there to much more complicated mathematics."

"I think you'd better stop there," says Milton, butting Archimedes in the chest for a stroke. "Before you lose us."

"But I love puzzles. You mustn't let maths worry you. If you follow the problem step by step then you don't get lost."

Answer: Donkey 5 Mule 7. You can work it out by guessing but there's a clever algebra answer too if you can work it out!

"I'll take your word for it," says Milton, looking unconvinced.

"But also sudden inspiration can produce an answer, can't it? You just see it, like how I did that mule and donkey puzzle." Harriet winks at Milton. "It's what you might call an Eureka moment."

"Eureka? The words for 'I have found it'? I'll have to remember that," muses Archimedes, making a note.

MEET THE SCIENTIST

ARCHIMEDES

- Lived: 287–212 BC
- Number of jobs: 3 (inventor, mathematician, engineer)
- Influence (out of 100): 75 (pioneer of practical science and first one to shout "Eureka!")
- Right? (out of 20): 18 (brilliant inventions including Archimedes's screw, burning mirrors to set enemy ships on fire, a mechanical claw to rip decks apart)
- Helpfully wrong? (out of 10): 0 (mostly right)
- Interesting death? (out of 10): 8 (killed by a soldier because he wouldn't leave his scientific puzzles to go and talk to the conquering Roman general, Marcellus)

THE FAMOUS EUREKA MOMENT!

After studying in Alexandria, Archimedes returned to Syracuse in Sicily and became the most famous scientist ever for making a sudden discovery. The story goes that he had been asked by the king to think up a method of checking if a crown had been made of pure gold as the craftsman claimed. As he couldn't melt it down to check the volume without ruining it, Archimedes had to come up with another way. Then one day he got in his bath and noticed that the water level rose. That prompted the thought that if he put the crown in a full bath and measured the water that was displaced he would work out the volume. He could then divide the mass of the crown by its volume and that would tell him if cheaper, lighter metals had been mixed in because he already knew how much that volume of gold should weigh.

So pleased was he by this brainwave that he jumped out of the bath and ran through the streets naked shouting "Eureka!"

And what happened when the crown was tested? It was found not to be pure and had silver mixed in. That bath got the craftsman into very hot water!

TRY THIS AT HOME:
MAKE YOUR OWN ARCHIMEDES SCREW

1. First gather what you need:
- 2 litre plastic bottle
- 1 wooden craft dowel about 30 cm long
- Heavyweight paper (scrapbook paper is ideal)
- Scissors
- Strong glue
- 1 drawing pin or tack
- A bowl of popcorn

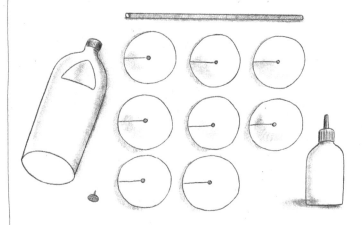

2. Cut off bottom of bottle.

3. Cut triangle shape out near neck, big enough so popcorn can enter at this point.

4. Take paper and cut out 8–10 disks a little smaller than diameter of bottle. Cut slit in each to the centre.

5. Thread the dowel through centre of each disk.

6. Now glue one end made by the slit to disk next to it. Repeat until you have a screw shape.

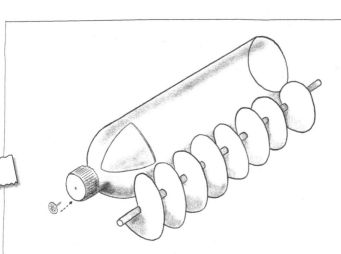

7. Push drawing pin through bottle lid so pin part goes inside cap. Now push end of dowel into the pin to fix it at that end. You should now have your completed Archimedes screw inside the bottle.

8. Put bottle into popcorn bowl and turn the screw. You should be able to see the popcorn being lifted up the bottle so you can eat it when it reaches the top. Enjoy!

WHAT ABOUT THE REST OF THE WORLD?

Harriet and Milton are following the story of science as it happened in the Western world. There were other places which were busy with their own inventions at the same time. Here are two of the most curious.

CHINESE SCIENCE

China and the Far East have their own long history of philosophy and technology. They were the first to record astronomical events like comets and solar eclipses. This also involved big picture thinking. The Chinese came up with the idea that all human affairs were governed by heaven (or Tian) and all their observatories were based on that idea. They were also the first to come up with the four key inventions: paper, printing, gunpowder, and the compass. These spread to the rest of the world, forever changing the way humans do things. We wouldn't have this book without them!

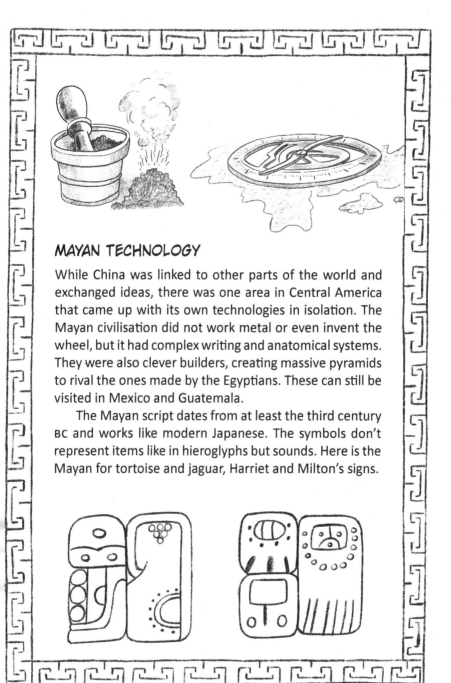

MAYAN TECHNOLOGY

While China was linked to other parts of the world and exchanged ideas, there was one area in Central America that came up with its own technologies in isolation. The Mayan civilisation did not work metal or even invent the wheel, but it had complex writing and anatomical systems. They were also clever builders, creating massive pyramids to rival the ones made by the Egyptians. These can still be visited in Mexico and Guatemala.

The Mayan script dates from at least the third century BC and works like modern Japanese. The symbols don't represent items like in hieroglyphs but sounds. Here is the Mayan for tortoise and jaguar, Harriet and Milton's signs.

BC TO AD

Leaving Archimedes to his studies, Harriet and Milton head back to the time machine.

"We're not changing locations on this journey," she explains, "but we are going forward to the new millennium."

"You mean we're going from BC, or Before Christ, to AD, Anno Domini, or Year of our Lord?" asks Milton.

"Yes, though some historians call it BCE and CE, Before the Common Era and Common Era."

"But what was thought to be the date of Jesus Christ's birth, 1 AD, is still the dividing point?"

"Yes, that's right," says Harriet. "Though different cultures and religions have their own calendars, this had become the standard one around the world."

Milton scratches his ear. "So what is different about Alexandria BC to AD?"

"To start with, it wasn't Christianity which didn't really take hold until centuries later," explains Harriet. "The biggest change was the rise of the Roman Empire. We've been visiting Greek scientists but perhaps, before we arrive, now is the moment to mention some famous ones from Rome."

BC

197 Rise of Roman Empire with victories over Greece

99 Birth of Lucretius

86 Roman General Sulla captures Athens

AD

10 Hero of Alexandria

23 Pliny the Elder

c. 33 Death of Jesus and beginning of Christianity

129 Birth of Galen

c. 150 Alexandrine astronomer Ptolemy
develops geocentric model of the heavens

c. 155 Birth of Tertullian of Carthage

267 The invading Goths sack
Athens and other Greek cities

c. 350 Birth of Hypatia

380 Christianity becomes official religion of Roman Empire

c. 490 Birth of John Philoponus and Simplicius

646 Final fall of Alexandria to Islamic rule and destruction of the
library

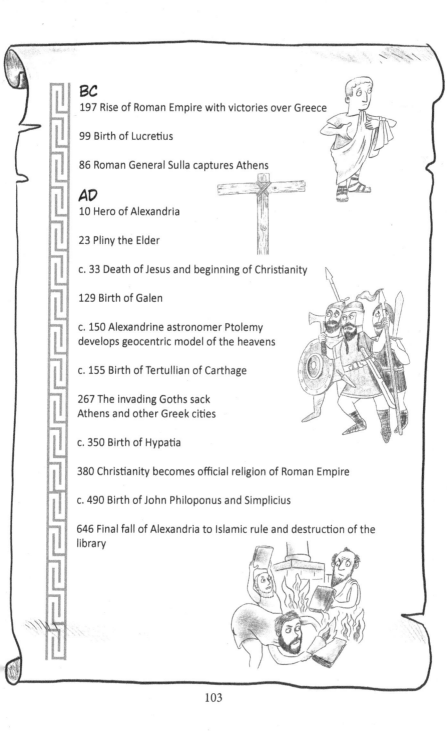

MEET THE SCIENTIST

LUCRETIUS

- Lived: c. 99–c. 44 BC
- Number of jobs: 2 (poet, philosopher)
- Influence (out of 100): 60 (handed on the Greek atomic idea to later generations in his poem "On the Nature of Things" and also the idea that chance rather than gods and goddesses was the force at work in nature)
- Right? (out of 20): 11 (important as a transmitter of ideas rather than original thinker)
- Helpfully wrong? (out of 10): 2 (little to judge him by)
- Interesting death? (out of 10): 6 (various stories, including one where he was driven mad by love potion and committed suicide – this was likely to have come from his enemies)

MEET THE SCIENTIST

GALEN, THE GLADIATORS' DOCTOR

- Lived: 129–c. 210 AD
- Number of jobs: 2 (doctor, including to gladiators of Pergamum, medical writer)
- Influence (out of 100): 95 (said the best doctors were philosophers and guided medical practice for centuries!)
- Right? (out of 20): 10 (right about treating medical problems with lifestyle changes – diet, exercise etc.)
- Helpfully wrong? (out of 10): 1 (banned fresh fruit and followed four humours idea which led to the spilling of much blood for future patients!)
- Interesting death? (out of 10): 1 (appears to have died of old age)

105

MEET THE SCIENTIST

PLINY THE ELDER

- Lived: 23–79 AD
- Number of jobs: 6 (Roman military officer, naval commander, historian, philosopher, naturalist, and scientific writer)
- Influence (out of 100): 55 (first to attempt to write an encyclopedia of all that was known about the natural world at the time, the model for all later attempts)
- Right? (out of 20): 14 (conveyed the knowledge of Roman world but less noted as an original thinker)
- Helpfully wrong? (out of 10): 0 (mostly got things right and was a great source for thinkers in his day)
- Interesting death? (out of 10): 8 (died in eruption of Vesuvius going to rescue his friends)

Harriet brings the time machine to a stop. "We're making a quick call in 50 AD to see one of science's best toy and machine makers."

"What's his name?" asks Milton.

"Hero of Alexandria. He was born just into the new era in 10 AD and lived for fifty years. He is thought to have taught at the Museum. He is proof that Greek science wasn't all theory. Some people were curious about inventing things. But be careful: you never know what's going to happen when you go into his workshop."

With that warning, Milton carefully nudges open the door of the time machine and ducks as a steam-powered rocket whizzes by.

"My Heron engine works! It really flies!" chuckles Hero, running to fetch his machine from where it landed.

Milton steps out into a workshop of wonders.

Heron Engine

Holy Water Dispenser

108

Wind-powered Organ

Automated Puppet
Show

"Do you like it?" asks Hero enthusiastically, so caught up in his device that he doesn't stop to ask where a tortoise and cat have suddenly appeared from.

"It's very... advanced," says Milton, wondering why steam power didn't catch on until so much later if Hero was playing with it eighteen centuries earlier.

"Such a wonderful toy," agrees Hero, straightening out a bend in the nose where it crash-landed.

That was probably why, Milton decides. Hero saw it as an interesting oddity rather than a machine that could do useful work.

"Would you like to see my wind-powered organ?" Hero sticks his head out the window. "Not enough wind today so we'll use bellows. Come on." He signals to his slave to start puffing the bellows. The breeze the slave produces turns a windmill, which works the organ. Little puppet birds open their mouths on the top of each pipe as Hero sits down to play. He is a terrible musician, making sounds like an elephant in distress, but Harriet and Milton smile politely.

"See! One day you won't even need organists to play music. It will just pour out of machines automatically," declares Hero.

Harriet and Milton exchange a look.

"Don't change the timeline," whispers Harriet.

"So it is all right for you to nudge Archimedes to shout 'Eureka!' but not to tell Hero about recorded music and computers?"

"Exactly."

Milton sighs. "Sometimes, Harriet, you are too big for your boots."

"I don't wear boots."

"Shell then," humphs Milton, "too big for your shell."

Hero leaps off the organ stool and dashes over to another machine. "Had enough music, eh? What about a drink?" He puts a coin in a slot which moves a lever and a serving of water comes out of a spout.

"He has just invented the vending machine," whispers Milton.

"I thought it would be useful for temples," Hero explains. "Get your holy water after the appropriate price has been paid. Soon we won't need temple attendants either."

"Who else is he planning to put out of a job?" Milton mutters.

"Would you like to see my play?" asks the inventor. Without waiting for an answer, he starts up an automated puppet show, worked by cogs and ropes and complete with thunder effects made by metal balls rolling in a drum. The performance lasts ten minutes and Hero laughs loudly at his own visual jokes. "Soon you won't need actors. You can have your own private entertainment at home, playing away in the corner."

"Don't!" Harriet warns Milton.

Milton flicks his tail in annoyance. "I was not going to mention television. I am just going to congratulate him." Milton jumps on to the inventor's lap, hoping to slow him down a little. "You are very clever, sir. How do you think up all these things?"

Hero strokes Milton. "Simple really. I really love mathematics and I just apply the principles I learn to mechanics. It is all about weights and measures, cogs and ropes, working out how to harness the power of nature, and thinking how to do things in new ways."

Milton purrs, rubbing his head against the inventor's arm in admiration.

"Thank you for the demonstration," says Harriet. "Milton, we'd better go before you decide to move in with Hero for good. Remember what they do to cats after death here."

"Not in 50 AD?" asks Milton, outraged.

"Yes, it's still going on."

Milton jumps quickly down. "Lovely to have met you, sir. Keep up the good work!"

Back in the time machine, Milton settles down in his cat basket. "I don't know about you, Harriet, but Hero is certainly *my* hero now. I love it when curiosity about how things work leads to practical inventions."

"Our next visit is less funny but equally important," explains Harriet. "We're off to meet the first female scientist of antiquity."

The two explorers get out of the time machine in 410 AD. They find themselves in the middle of a lecture in one of the theatres. Ranks of eager students are sitting on the benches. Instead of a man in the chair, a woman is addressing them, teaching the ideas of Plato and Aristotle.

"She's the headteacher," whispers Harriet. "Her name is Hypatia."

"How did she get to be in charge?" asks Milton. "I thought women weren't allowed an education at this time."

Harriet nods. "That's right, but she was the daughter of a celebrated mathematician who saw how bright she was and so he sent her to school in Athens. She learnt all the most up-to-date ideas in philosophy, mathematics, and astronomy. She was so impressive that she was made head of the school in Alexandria in around 400 AD."

"That's pretty awesome."

"We won't disturb her," says Harriet, getting back in the time machine. "Unfortunately, her story has an unhappy end. In 415, she got caught up in a dispute between the local governor and bishop. She was killed by a Christian mob, partly it is thought because she was a famous person in the city and a pagan."

"So is this one of those moments when faith clashes with science?" asks Milton, feeling very sad now he knows how the story ends.

"I don't think so. Hypatia wasn't killed for her scientific ideas, but because local politics turned ugly. As a woman in authority, she was a target."

"There's nothing funny about that." Milton looks out on Alexandria, his whiskers drooping.

"No, I did warn you."

"So did science end badly in Alexandria?"

"It did have one final flourishing before the library and schools were destroyed," says Harriet. "Let's go forward to our last stop in 530."

THE FORGOTTEN HERO OF SCIENCE

Peering out of the porthole, Milton is excited to see Alexandria in the middle of the first millennium. "So by now they must have stopped mummifying cats?" he asks hopefully.

Harriet smiles. "You'd be surprised. Alexandria like the rest of the Mediterranean world at that time is a mix of different traditions, all fighting it out in debates in the lecture halls and sometimes more bloodily on the streets. But they line up in these two main groups."

Harriet's Guide to Alexandria c. 500 AD: Mid-Millennium Mayhem

Schools of Plato and Aristotle:

> i) We retell traditional stories of our gods in light of science

> ii) We treat the cosmos and heavens as eternal and divine

> iii) Change only happens on earthly sphere below the moon sphere

Abrahamic faiths in 500 AD: Judaism and Christianity:

> i) God created the world so the universe is not eternal

> ii) God stands outside creation but sets the rules for it

> iii) The purpose of our scientific study is to discover and enjoy those rules

"They sound pretty far apart," says Milton.

Harriet nods. "Some writers tried to find common ground. The writer of John's gospel, which is one of the books in the New Testament, starts 'In the beginning was the word' which in Greek is 'logos'. He was trying to build a bridge to Greek Philosophy, the kind of ideas we saw debated in Miletus centuries before."

"So what happened next?" asks Milton.

"Not what you would expect. I'm afraid the good guy doesn't win."

"Boo! But I'm beginning to expect the unexpected on this adventure."

"And right now I'm going to introduce you to a forgotten hero of science." Harriet smiles.

"Does he have a hero type name? Super Science Man? Big Thought?"

"He is called John Philoponus."

"Philoponus? Is that Greek for Super Man?" Milton asks, hopefully.

"No," laughs Harriet. "His name means 'lover of hard work'."

"So he's a Super Swot?"

Harriet nudges him. "Nothing wrong with studying hard. All of these people we've been meeting did that because they found the thing they loved to do. Like us and our time travelling."

"Fair point."

They exit the time machine in the courtyard of the Museum.

"Where is Super Swot?" asks Milton.

"Oh no! Up there!" squawks Harriet.

Milton looks up and finds John above them standing on top of the building. He has two rocks in his hands.

"Look out below!" John shouts as he drops them.

Harriet disappears inside her shell while Milton leaps out of the way.

The scientist hurries down to them. "Sorry about that. I checked
the courtyard earlier and it was empty. You didn't get hurt, did
you?"

"No, it missed me," says Harriet from inside her shell. "Just."

"What were you doing?" hisses Milton, his fur stuck up on end.
"What idiot drops things from the roof just for fun? I thought you
were a swot! I thought you were supposed to be stuck inside with
your books!"

John strokes Milton to calm him. "Sorry, little cat. But study
isn't just about reading the work of other people. Once you've
done that you have to go out and test what they write. So did you
see which one landed first?"

"No," says Harriet, her head still hidden. "But is it safe now?"

"Yes, yes, quite safe."

"I saw," says Milton. "They landed at the same time."

John claps his hands. "Exactly what I saw when I got a student to drop the stones yesterday." He picks them up. "See, they are different weights. This one is much bigger and heavier. If Aristotle is right then this one should fall faster and hit the ground first."

"But it doesn't," says Milton.

"That's right. But I'm finding it very hard to persuade my colleagues even to look at my experiments because they all think Aristotle can't be wrong.

"Come into my study. You deserve a dish of milk and a lettuce leaf for your scare."

They follow him into his room where he rummages in a cupboard and finds the treats for them.

"You're not going to mummify me, are you?" Milton sniffs the milk suspiciously.

"Of course not!" laughs John. "I'm a Christian, not one of the followers of the old Egyptian gods."

"Are there many of them around here still?" asks Harriet, her words slightly mumbled as her mouth is full of lettuce.

"Not so many in the school. We have Jews and Christians and there are a large number of students here who follow Greek philosophical traditions. We don't always see eye to eye."

"And I suppose that's why they don't like you saying Aristotle is wrong?" suggests Milton.

"Exactly," sighs John. "And my own side aren't that keen either. I get a lot of them telling me off for asking questions.

Tertullian of Carthage
c. 155–240 AD

We have no need of curiosity since Jesus Christ.

"The good news is that I also get encouragement from other Christians who think differently. They think that many streams flow into the way of truth, including scientific ones found in other traditions. That's what Clement thought. He was around at the same time as Tertullian. Clement used to teach here too so I've got a good example to follow."

John sits down and lets Milton jump onto his lap. "That's better now, isn't it? Am I forgiven?"

"Yes," purrs Milton.

"What other mistakes have you spotted in Aristotle?" asks Harriet.

"The idea that the air pushes a spear from behind? Well, that's just not right if you test it. I think motion results from the original push given by the person who throws. That impetus carries the spear as far as it can before it is exhausted or it hits the target. The really exciting thing if you follow that thought is that it means motion can happen in a vacuum without the presence of air to do the 'pushing.'"

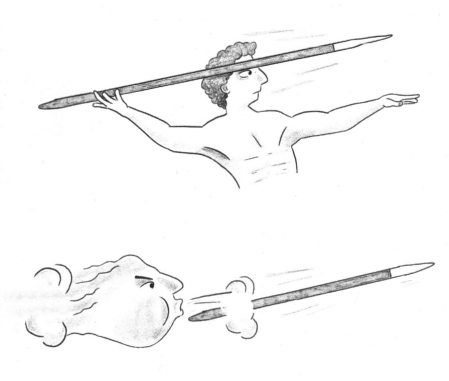

"It's very clever of you to work that out," says Harriet.

"Thank you. But I can't get my colleagues to agree," says John. "They believe Aristotle is such a major thinker that they daren't challenge his ideas. They've told me to shut up about science and stick to teaching grammar."

"You mustn't let them silence you!" protests Harriet. "You are right!"

"And they really don't like it when I suggest the world isn't eternal and that the heavens are made of the same stuff as Earth."

The door bangs open and another teacher in the school walks in. "What are you all doing in here?"

John gets to his feet, ready for another fight.

SIMPLICIUS V PHILOPONUS

I win - you used impetus to move your fist!

"Who are you?" asks Milton, miffed that they've been interrupted so rudely and he has lost a warm lap on which to curl up.

"Simplicius of Cilicia," says the man proudly. "And you are?"

"Harriet of Darwin and Milton of Schrödinger," says Milton with matching pride. "Travellers in…"

"In this very interesting part of the world," Harriet says quickly before he can mention the time machine.

"You shouldn't listen to John here. We must keep Aristotle's idea of the perfect, eternal universe above the moon."

"Why?" asks Harriet.

"Because… because it's what he said and what we've all thought ever since!'

Harriet frowns. "Have you tested it?"

"How can we?" asks Simplicius, looking exasperated. "We live here on the Earth. Just look up. The stars may move but they don't change. That means the heavens are perfect and eternal. These Christians like John think God created the world but I can see no sign of a starting point."

"But Simplicius, your heroes, Plato and Aristotle, don't always agree," argues John. "Aristotle himself says that there can't be an infinity of things. That means the universe can't be eternal as it has limits."

"Twaddle!" Simplicius slams the door on the way out.

"Ah well," says John, sitting down at his desk. "I don't think we'll ever agree. It's like when I try to talk about the book of Genesis to my friends. The followers of Greek philosophy don't like the idea of creation and a God involved in the physical world in that way and my more unbending Christian friends take it all literally, that it took seven days and happened exactly as described."

"And what do you think?" asks Harriet.

"I think Genesis describes the fact of God's creation but not how it came about. That leaves room for me to make scientific investigation to solve that mystery."

Harriet smiles. "So you have plenty of room for curiosity about the natural world alongside your belief in God?"

"It's even better than that," explains John. "Knowing that God created the world inspires me to study it. Now, how am I going to create a vacuum to test my theory about motion?"

Leaving John to his thinking, Harriet and Milton get back in the time machine.

"Harriet, I thought it was Galileo in the sixteenth century who was the one who overturned Aristotle's theory of falling weights by dropping things off the Tower of Pisa?"

"Yes, he gets the credit in most history books but John arrived at the idea first. His works weren't very well known though so his ideas didn't have a chance to catch on. That was because he seemed so bold in suggesting Aristotle was wrong. It is one of our 'uh-oh' moments with the Greek philosophical thinkers getting in the way of John's scientific discoveries.

Uh-oh!

"Galileo did know of John though, so possibly that helped him all those centuries later when he started asking questions." Harriet looks at the time dial. "So I suppose we need to go and ask him."

"Is that the next stop on our Curiosity Quest?"

"Yes, I think it is. But wait a moment: I just need to clean the porthole window. All this Alexandrian sea salt and sand has made it dirty."

Harriet steps outside with her spotted red handkerchief and begins to wipe the glass. As Milton watches, a hand comes down and plucks her from the ground.

"Excellent. Just what I wanted for my studies!" declares Simplicius as he runs off with her.

"Harriet!" squawks Milton, scampering outside.

But he is too late. Harriet has been tortoise-napped.

"Don't worry, Harriet: I'll save you!" vows Milton. "This thing must have a tracking device!" He dashes inside the time machine to set off in pursuit.

It is going to be a very rocky ride if our time travellers are ever going to reach Galileo!

Where to go to find out more

There are lots of helpful websites that will tell you more about the people, objects, and places mentioned in Milton and Harriet's quest. Here are a few to start you on your own curiosity quest.

Ready to do some stargazing? First check out the phase of the moon at http://www.moonconnection.com/moon_phases_calendar.phtml

Then find out what the stars are doing where you are tonight: http://astronomynow.com/uk-sky-chart/

Want to find out more about the Greek world? You can go to http://www.bbc.co.uk/schools/primaryhistory/ancient_greeks/greek_world/

Like to try more experiments? There are many excellent suggestions on the web. Start at http://www.sciencekids.co.nz/experiments.html or https://sciencebob.com/category/experiments/

Curious about maths? Try www.wild.maths.org (for students) or www.nrich.maths.org (for teachers)

Want to find out more about Chinese science? http://www.historyforkids.net/ancient-chinese-science.html

Mayan writing: write your own name in Mayan script at www.paleoaliens.com/event/mayan_glyphs/

How about visiting the Seven Wonders of the ancient World? http://easyscienceforkids.com/all-about-the-seven-wonders-of-the-ancient-world/

Want to discover more about the first famous female scientist, Hypatia? http://kids.britannica.com/elementary/article-399865/Hypatia

Answers

How many times did you spot the Curiosity Bug? The answer is 16.

Did you draw the lines in the puzzle on page 63 like this?

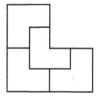

For other puzzles visit http://brainden.com/geometry-puzzles.htm

Meet the authors

Julia Golding is a multi-award-winning children's novelist, including the Cat Royal Series and the Companions Quartet. Having given up on science at sixteen, she became interested again when she realized just how inspiring science can be. It really does tell the best stories! This is her first experiment with non-fiction but hopefully her collaborators, Roger and Andrew, will prevent any laboratory accidents.

Andrew Briggs is the professor of nanomaterials at the University of Oxford. Nanomaterials just means small stuff. In his laboratory he studies problems like how electricity flows through a single molecule (you can't get stuff much smaller than a single molecule). He is also curious about big questions. He flies aeroplanes, but he has never been in a time travel machine like the one that Harriet and Milton use—yet!

Roger Wagner is an artist who paints power stations and angels (among other things) and has work in collections around the world. He didn't do the drawings for these books, but like Milton and Harriet he wanted to find out how the 'big picture' thinking of artists, was connected to what scientists do. When he met Andrew Briggs the two of them set out on a journey to answer that question. Their journey (which they described in a book called The Penultimate Curiosity) was almost (but not quite) as exciting as Milton and Harriet's.

Harriet and Milton continue
their quest in

ROCKY ROAD
TO GALILEO

– coming soon!